MW00887644

TO THE ICE

Dedicated to the polar explorers
Fridtjof Nansen and Ernest Shackleton

Thomas Tidholm
Anna-Clara Tidholm

Translated by Julia Marshall

GECKO PRESS

There were three of us:
Jack, Max and me, Ida.
This is what happened to us.
You might not believe it's true,
and we didn't believe it ourselves,
not even while it was happening.

But this is how it was…

CHAPTER 1

WE FLOAT AWAY

I T WAS A SATURDAY, I think. We'd decided to go to the creek. Our side was covered in thick snow, and we had to bounce our way through it. We used to go fishing there. There was a summer house and an old jetty. But now spring had begun and the creek had grown into a river with a lot of water. Big ice floes were sailing down it but some thick ice still clung to the bank.

Jack thought he saw otter tracks and walked gingerly out on the ice.

"Come back!" said Max.

"It'll hold," Jack said.

I followed him.

"Look, it's holding," I said.

So Max came out too, though you could see he was afraid. He brought a branch with him.

Once he was on the ice, we stood still and looked into the black water. There was a quiet crack. Then the entire sheet broke loose and began to move. Max started yelling.

We all yelled, but it was too late. There was no time to jump ashore. The ice floe was drifting away, slowly and almost elegantly. It spun a little at first, but then it sailed on like a boat.

We stood absolutely still; we didn't dare to move. We weren't going all that fast, but soon the old jetty was out of sight. We drifted to the middle of the river. There were trees on both sides, but we couldn't reach them. Other floes, large and small, drifted around us.

We kept on floating downstream. There wasn't only ice, but a lot of debris too, all kinds of things. We managed to grab hold of a wooden box, using Max's branch. We pulled it up and sat on it. That meant we didn't have to sit directly on the ice.

The river grew wider and wider. Then it flowed into a bigger river, which also grew and grew. Finally, we couldn't see the riverbanks, just a bit of land in one direction. We couldn't see any more birds.

We didn't know where we were.

Jack said he thought a boat would come along. We'd wave, and they'd pick us up and we'd sit on deck, wrapped in blankets and drinking hot chocolate. But we didn't see a boat.

Then it started snowing. Now no one would be able to see us anyway.

When it stopped snowing, we realized that we were far out in the middle of nowhere. All around us was just ice and water. But then the sun came out from behind a cloud and everything was washed in bright soft light, like a painting. It was changing constantly. It was quite beautiful, even though we were scared.

Max tasted the water. It was a little bit salty.

"We're at sea now," said Jack. "The Ice Sea, maybe. I've read about it. It's very big."

"The Ice Sea, that's a long way away," I said.

"Well, it's a sea with ice in it, anyway," said Jack.

We'd been drifting for hours now and it was getting dark. Our ice floe floated slowly and delicately onwards, and more and more floes gathered around us. The moon came shining up, big and round, and kept us company. There actually is a man in the moon, even though we hadn't planned to meet him on this particular night.

I think we slept a little on our box, leaning against each other. When we woke up it was bright, bright and the sun was rising. But there was a new chill in the air.

Our ice floe had frozen together with lots of others; it had become a kind of ice floor with just a little snow on top. Wherever we turned, it looked the same.

"I want to go home now," said Max.

When we tried to remember which way was home, everyone had a different idea. So Max got to decide.

We began walking towards the sun. It seemed a good idea because home was probably in that direction.

You can tell which way north and south are by looking at the sun when the clock says twelve. Jack actually had a watch, but he reckoned it wasn't right. We understood then that this was going to be hard work at the very least, and we soon found that the ice wasn't smooth at all. Sometimes we had to jump over water.

It became harder and harder to walk, and also colder. A strong wind blew.

Up ahead, the ice had been compressed into rugged hills, sharp shards of ice shoved up on their edges.

"It's pack ice," said Jack. "I've read about it. Too bad I forgot to bring my new phone, it even has a compass."

"Yes, but you can bring it next time," I said.

We walked all day, occasionally resting a little. We didn't say anything then, just breathed, because you can't say anything if you don't know anything and you're only wondering to yourself the whole time, what's going to happen? We got tired and sweaty and frozen. Finally, we couldn't walk any further.

Strange, but we hadn't realized till now that we were hungry. Unbelievably hungry. And that I had sandwiches! I took them out of my backpack, and we drank the tea I'd brought in a thermos. As we sat there, it grew darker.

"Was that all the food we had?" Jack asked.

"I have three more sandwiches," I said.

We crept in between blocks of ice, which made a kind of cave. We huddled together and tried to sleep.

The sky outside was like flames of red, blue and green sweeping over the sky, long bright ribbons that appeared and disappeared.

"It's the aurora," said Jack. "Those are electrons coming from the sun."

Jack had obviously read about that too, but none of us had seen it before, so we had to climb up on a block of ice to watch. We felt very small.

The next day we kept walking. We were having a rest when suddenly we saw land in the far distance. What country could that be? It looked like black cliffs. With no trees growing. Nothing.

CHAPTER 2

WINTER AND DARKNESS

WE KEPT WALKING, and the land we'd seen drew nearer. It was blacker than black, but behind the black rose a wall of ice, white and gleaming.

"This isn't home…" Max said. And he began to cry.

Jack and I comforted him as best we could, but of course we were scared too, and disappointed.

There was water close to the shore, but there were also ice floes we could use for steps.

We jumped ashore and searched until we found a crevice in the mountainside, out of the wind. We crept in there together.

How can three frozen people get warm? By lying close together, like puzzle pieces. It may sound strange, but you can actually warm up that way.

I was still freezing, though, and I couldn't sleep. Sometime in the night I heard shuffling outside, as if something big were moving out there. And suddenly there was something, darkening the entrance to the cave. A huge shadow! Then it disappeared, but I heard the shuffling again, big shuffling steps. I crawled over and looked out.

Someone was standing there. It looked like a big…penguin! I had never seen a real penguin.

Or…was it a penguin? It was far too big. But its white chest shone in the dark and you could see its big, curved beak against the sky. It looked down at me. Or it seemed to. And I was scared.

But then it seemed to point one wing up towards the mountain. Then it went on up itself, setting its feet on big stones, jumping between boulders. Finally, it disappeared over a ledge.

Next morning, I told the others about it. Jack laughed and said: "You dreamed it! There aren't any penguins that big."

"Maybe we're dreaming everything," I said.

We ate our last sandwiches. But then, instead of sitting and feeling homesick and sorry for ourselves, we decided to climb the slope.

Strangely, there was a kind of path through the massive boulders. It was still very hard going, and we had to stop many times. After a while we could see out over the great sea of ice where we'd been walking yesterday. It stretched all the way to the horizon.

Higher up, we came to a flat bit of land. And there was a house! One of the world's smallest and most dilapidated houses. Maybe more of a hut. But still.

That's what the great penguin had wanted to show us, I thought. But I didn't see any gigantic penguin tracks, and I didn't say anything.

Yes, it was a tiny, dilapidated house, but it had a roof and walls. And a door that wasn't quite closed. Snow had come in.

Inside, everything looked very old and was covered in dust.

"People have lived here," said Max.

"Yes, a long time ago," I said.

"Look, they've left food behind!" said Jack.

There were large tin cans lining a wall. There was a stove, there were bunks with old mattresses and skins, and here and there various tools, saws and hatchets, broken and rusty. Also several strange things we didn't know what to do with. On a table was a book that someone had written in with pencil.

"Let's hope we can open these tins," said Jack.

There we were: Jack, Max and me, Ida. The three of us now lived in this little broken-down house. It was just as well we had it because outside it was much colder. And we had nowhere else to go. Outside the wind howled, but inside there was almost none at all. That was the best thing. It was really good!

We went around and looked at everything, rummaging in the rubble and searching for something to open the tins. We had to use a saw.

We wanted to stay inside as much as we could, but the toilet had to be out in the snow. We lit the fire with pieces of wood from one wall and warmed ourselves, along with some tins. There were fish balls in every one of them! Then we found a sack of dried leaves. We decided it was tea. We melted snow and boiled it.

"Where have they hidden the sugar?" asked Max.

We slept under piles of skins and old furs.

Of course, we were worried and afraid, but if anyone lay awake crying then none of us could sleep. In the end, we decided that everyone who wanted to should cry at the same time, all together. After a few days everyone stopped crying and we slept quite well.

We had so, so much time. It was as if time didn't exist anymore. The most important thing when that happens, and you don't know how long it will last, is to know how to be bored! It's an art to be able to wait when there's nothing to wait for. Animals know how to: cats, for example, just sit and might not be thinking about anything at all. It's a good talent. But people think so much all the time that our heads get hot.

Every morning, once it was a tiny bit light outside, we woke and told each other our dreams. And if we couldn't remember, we made them up. We laughed a lot. Those were our best moments. That's how we started each day.

Jack and Max were brothers. They'd brought along some old squabbles from home, which they carried on so they had something to do when it got dark. I had to get used to hearing them argue under their blanket.

Things were actually pretty terrible. What would happen, how would we get out of there, what if we went crazy?

Of course, we didn't want to think about those things. So we didn't. We sort of removed them without talking about them. Somehow, we made everything almost normal. And when everything is normal, you can do anything you want.

Here's a list of things you can do if you happen to be trapped in a tiny hut in the snow in the middle of nowhere:

Sit and talk to yourself, dance around with your clothes back to front, or take them off and decorate yourself using pieces of charcoal.

Draw pictures on the walls, sing old songs you learned in school and never cared about before.

Pretend to be a stranger who comes in and asks the way to the shop.

Try to fix something unfixable.

Sleep when you get tired, or tired of the others.

Play rock, paper, scissors and play rock, paper, scissors again and then play more rock, paper, scissors.

And be bored.

We taught ourselves to walk on our hands. Then we learned how to braid each other's hair. We got quite good at it. We'd all grown long hair!

If we'd ever been shy with each other, that was over now.

The only thing we were strict about was dinner. Then we'd say to each other:

"Max, would you pass me another fish ball please?"

"Jack, would you like a fish ball perhaps?"

"No thank you, Ida, but do help yourself!"

We had so many fish balls.

"I think we're actually in a movie," said Max.

I thought, I hope it's called *The Return of the Great Penguin*. I dreamed often about the penguin—that he would come and rescue us. But more and more, it seemed likely he'd disappeared.

I wished I'd brought even one book with me, preferably a nice thick one. But since I hadn't, I started reading the old book. When I'd blown away the dust, I realized it was a diary from Lars Iversen's polar expedition! It was written by hand, with a lot of smudges, but I could read most of it.

It began: *We departed from London 1897 in the month of May on the three-masted sailing ship* Fremskritt.

Imagine, so long ago. They were going to study penguins. But it didn't go so well, and the ship sank. *We must now leave the ship, which is stuck irretrievably in the ice and will be crushed.*

Iversen had made it to shore with his three shipmates. They'd built this little hut using wood from the ship. They'd soon had enough of penguins. *For three years we have waded all the long winter through snow, and all summer through penguin dung.*

I could almost see them sitting in here, eating their fish balls, just like us. Bearded and bedraggled, tough-looking types. Or maybe sick and miserable. More than a hundred years ago. But they must have been rescued because they were no longer here. Maybe a boat came at last, and they were in such a hurry to get away, they forgot the diary. Or did they leave it for us, so we could learn what happened?

The last entry in the book said: *We now leave this desolate place where we have spent three wretched years. May no one experience what we have been through!*

No, who would want to? Not us.

But at the very end, it said: *We survived. Only because we wanted to live.*

Of course, I thought. Thanks for the tip!

I don't know how long we lived in the little house. There were many days the same, with noughts and crosses and fish balls and songs and stories about people we knew and tears and homesickness and darkness. Outside everything was covered in snow and more snow. The hut included.

Every evening we heard the sound of a plane, way, way above. Maybe the people inside were on the way to a far-off island with sun and warm beaches. They were drinking wine and laughing and had no idea that we were down here.

After about a hundred years, the days became lighter, almost as if it were spring! We hardly believed it but the days went on brightening. The sun was up in the sky again, and more and more birds came flying in from the sea.

One morning the entire beach below us was full of penguins. Masses of penguins! There was chattering and screeching everywhere, as if life had returned!

"Great to have company," said Max.

We were pleased. We went outside, the sky was blue! We decided to celebrate Easter. But we had to celebrate Christmas first, Max reckoned, because we'd forgotten that. So we had them both at the same time. With a real snowball fight! We'd found a few jars of marmalade, so we ate that for dessert after the fish balls. Then everything became a bit more like a party because sometimes it doesn't take much.

"Plus, there are vitamins in marmalade, and that's important," said Jack.

CHAPTER 3

TO SEA AGAIN

THE WIND OFTEN BLEW. But then one night a real storm arrived that tugged and tore at our old house until it began to groan and shriek. We had to run outside and shelter in a hollow. And when it became light, our hut was no longer there, just a huge pile of posts and planks.

"We can build a boat," I said, "and row home."

Max and Jack agreed.

Of course, building a boat is not easy, especially if you've never done it before. But you can do it if you badly want to. We had to start over again several times. It took a long while, because we were figuring it out as we built.

We got it looking almost like a boat, but there were gaps everywhere. We had to seal them with fish balls and penguin poop and seaweed and then nail boards over the gaps.

We called the boat *Homeward*.

"Once it's in the water the boards will swell and make it watertight," said Jack. "I've read about that."

Then we lowered the boat to the beach using a thick rope.

There were quite a few penguins on the shore, and two of them decided to live in the boat. They didn't want to move, they liked it so much. So, okay, we dragged it into the water, penguins and all.

We took a supply of fish balls and a jar of marmalade. We raised the mast and pushed the boat out.

We were on our way!

Jack and I took turns to row. Max was too short; he couldn't reach. Rowing was something new to learn, but eventually our arms got the hang of it and the boat moved in the direction we wanted.

Our boat floated fine! We set off between the ice floes. Fat seals lay all around, burping fish and ignoring us. It was the most beautiful day in the world, and we cheered because we were so happy. Birds of all kinds flew above us, almost hanging in the air and crying. It sounded like Gooodbyeeee!

But I never saw the great penguin again. If I had, I would have called out, "Thanks for helping!"

He wasn't there, though. And I'd begun to think it must have been a dream.

At first, we followed the steep coastline with its tall cliffs of ice, skyscrapers of ice. The sun shone on the ice so it shimmered blue and green. Water was running everywhere, like waterfalls.

Everything was huge! We stopped rowing and just looked. Enormous blocks of ice weighing ten thousand tons fell into the water and become icebergs. They sent great swells out to sea.

I dozed in the sun then woke to see ice floes in the distance. There seemed to be people standing on them and drifting slowly by. I thought about people who had to leave their homes to travel across vast oceans, without knowing how anything would turn out for them. But they didn't travel on ice floes, did they? And the next time I looked there were no people. Penguins stood on the floes nearby, completely still. Jack sat and rowed, and Max took a lick of marmalade and went back to sleep. Our own penguins had disappeared.

We'd reached the open sea when the sky suddenly turned black.

It was a storm! It thundered towards us in a great dark wall. It tossed our little boat here and there, down into the troughs and up to the foaming crests. We could do nothing but yell, hold on and hope for the best.

None of us had experienced anything like this before. To be terrified, to think that it's all over, that you're actually going to die, not later, not some other time, but this very moment!

And this very moment then stretches out into a whole long horror movie.

The waves crashed over us and the boat groaned. Jack's face was snow-white, Max threw up, and I… wet myself. You have to pee at some point, and I guess that was it.

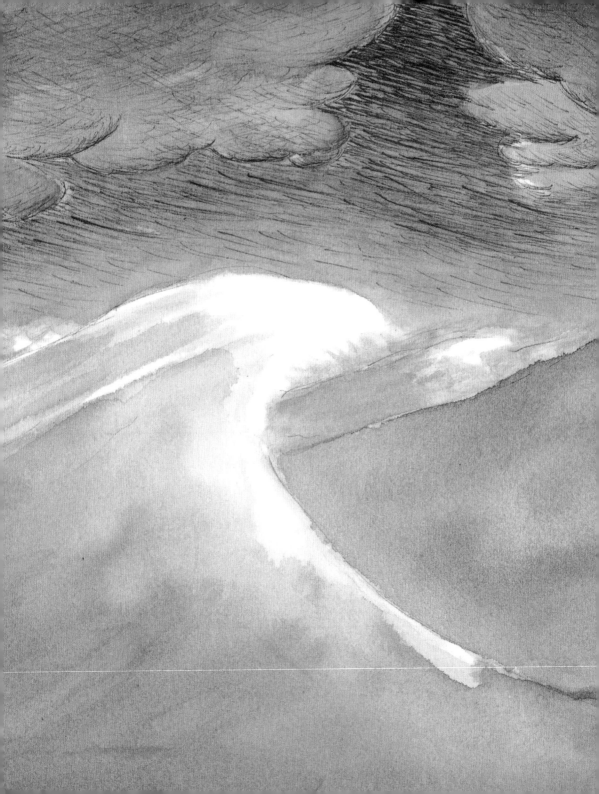

But it all turned out alright. The fact that the boat held together, we could hardly believe.

When the storm had passed, it was absolutely calm. The wind had carried us far out, away from the coast, away from the cliffs and the ice.

Soon we had an ordinary gentle wind again. We raised a sail and the boat sped forward.

"Shall we go home now?" asked Max. "I liked it in our little house."

"Do you want to turn around?" Jack said.

"And the penguins…" said Max.

"The house blew down," said Jack. "Don't you remember?"

Max didn't say any more.

We sailed for many hours, maybe days, for as long as it took to go from one world to a completely different one.

And then we saw in the far distance a coast that came closer and closer. Trees were growing on it, firs and birches and pines. We knew where we were!

We tipped the last fish balls overboard. We never wanted to eat those again.

And soon we were sailing up the river, which became a creek. Home!

It was still spring, but now the snow had disappeared—and the ice. Some green was showing along the banks, and those little yellow flowers. We stayed quiet in the boat.

There was our old jetty.

The three of us had come home again: Jack, Max and me, Ida. Our journey was over. We looked at each other. What should we do now?

"We'd better go home," said Jack. "They've probably been worried."

"Do you think so?" I said.

"But what shall we say if they ask where we've been?" asked Max.

"Tell the truth," I said. "That we don't know."

"No, we know it was a long way away," said Max. "A long, long way away."

"Yes, we know that much," Jack said. "And we also learned some other things."

"Mostly about ice," said Max. "There was a lot of ice there."

We hugged and said, see you.

And then off they went.

When they'd gone, I pushed the boat out. It floated slowly down the creek. We didn't need it anymore. Besides, it was treacherous.

But thank you, little boat, you did a great job!

I stood a moment and watched it sail away.

I thought, one day…one day, I'll write a book about this adventure.

The End

This edition first published in 2023 by Gecko Press
PO Box 9335, Wellington 6141, Aotearoa New Zealand
office@geckopress.com

English-language edition © Gecko Press Ltd 2023
Translation © Julia Marshall 2023
© 2020 text Thomas Tidholm
© 2020 illustrations Anna-Clara Tidholm
First published by Alfabeta Bokförlag AB with the Swedish title *Isresan*

All rights reserved. No part of this publication may be reproduced or transmitted
or utilized in any form, or by any means, electronic, mechanical, photocopying or
otherwise, without the prior written permission of the publisher.

The author and illustrator assert their moral right to be identified as the author
and illustrator of the work.

Gecko Press aims to publish with a low environmental impact. Our books are
printed using vegetable inks on FSC-certified paper from sustainably managed
forests. We produce books of high quality with sewn bindings and beautiful
paper—made to be read over and over.

The cost of this translation was supported by a subsidy from the Swedish
Arts Council, gratefully acknowledged.

Original language: Swedish
Edited by Penelope Todd
Design by Megan van Staden
Printed in China by Everbest Printing Co. Ltd, an accredited ISO 14001
& FSC-certified printer

ISBN 9781776575077
Ebook available

For more curiously good books, visit geckopress.com